This ever so good book belongs to:

_____

_____

_____

For four wonderful grandparents from
their favourite granddaughter – GC

For Lucy who has the shiniest
golden locks – KC

4 North Parade | Bath UK | BA1 1LF
+44(0) 1225 310107
www.nppbooks.co.uk

Rapunzel
and her
Ever So Shiny
Locks

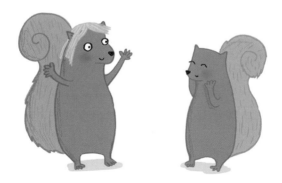

Written by Gemma Cary
Illustrated by Kelly Caswell

Once upon a time, there was a beautiful young lady called Rapunzel.

"Beautiful? Is that all?" says Rapunzel.

OK, let's start again ... Once there was a **beautiful, stunning, dazzling** young lady called Rapunzel.

"Much better!" says Rapunzel.

She lived in a tall tower where no one could bother her, and she spent all day taking care of her award-winning hair.

"I can skip with my hair."

"I can swing from it!"

"I can hide in it."

"My hair is the most marvellous hair **IN THE WORLD**!"

Rapunzel knew that, one day, a Prince would arrive at her tower. She also knew he would want to climb up, using her hair as a rope.

One morning, while Rapunzel was straightening her strands for the trillionth time, some hoofs came to a halt beneath her window.

"Rapunzel, Rapunzel! Let down your hair!" called the Prince.

"No, thanks," she replied.

"Rapunzel, Rapunzel! Let down your **ever so shiny** locks!"

"Not good enough."

"Rapunzel, Rapunzel! Let down your **ever so shiny, gorgeously golden, amazingly lustrous** locks!"

"Better ... but I'm still not putting my lovely hair out of the window. And I'm certainly not letting you put your dirty feet on it! Go away, Princey!"

"**Fine!**" said the Prince. "But I won't come back!"
After lots of tutting and humphing, he led his horse
away from the tower and galloped off.

"I don't need a **smelly old prince**," said Rapunzel, stroking her silky hair. "I'm perfectly fine on my own." And to prove it, she spent the rest of the day ironing her certificates and polishing her trophies.

Best Hair

1st

Weeks and months went by. The Prince rescued some other
beautiful maiden and their wedding was broadcast all over the world.

Rapunzel watched in silence. She wasn't jealous of the bride's elegant dress. She wasn't jealous of her sparkling tiara. She was jealous of all their friends.

For the first time in her life, Rapunzel felt lonely.

Rapunzel turned to the bird on her window sill.

"Birdie," she said, **"can you find me a friend**?"

The bird glared at Rapunzel. "My name,"she replied, "is Sylvia. And who would be friends with you? Nobody wants a friend who is vain and selfish."

Tears filled Rapunzel's eyes. "You're right, Sylvia," she said.

After eating some ice cream and watching her favourite film, Rapunzel felt a bit better.

"What should I do, Sylvia?" she asked, licking an enormous spoon.

"You need to prove to everyone that you've changed, Rapunzel. You should do something completely selfless. I suggest you cut off your hair."

"Cut off my hair? My **ever so shiny, gorgeously golden, amazingly lustrous** locks?"

"Yes," said Sylvia. "Cut it off and give it away."

Rapunzel took her best scissors. With trembling hands, she made a quick **snip**, then another, and another. Her hair tumbled to the floor.

Sylvia called to her friends and each bird swooped in to collect a **shimmering** lock of hair.

"What will it be used for?" asked Rapunzel.

"All sorts of things," replied Sylvia mysteriously, and she too flew off.

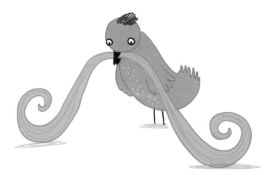

Before long, the hair was all gone. Rapunzel's neck felt cold. A **terrible** thought suddenly struck her! Without her hair, how would anyone climb up the tower to visit her? How would she ever make any friends? Rapunzel curled up and wept.

That night, Sylvia returned with birds of all colours, shapes and sizes. They gently lifted Rapunzel from her bed and carried her out of the tower. They **soared** over a deep forest and were soon **gliding** towards a glittering town.

From the sky, Rapunzel spotted long golden strands decorating the houses. She saw golden ribbons looped through the trees. Even the birds' nests were woven with **threads of gold**.

Faces **peeped** and **peered** to catch a glimpse of the girl who had made their town so special.

Rapunzel looked at the **wonderful** world around her.

"Welcome," said Sylvia, "to your new home."

Rapunzel never returned to her tower. And she never won another award for her hair. But the golden town attracted hundreds of visitors and Rapunzel soon made lots of friends. And that made her **ever so smiley**.